D1742857

LEAD ME TO THE WEIRD PLACES

A Hermit's Book of Madness

Joel Dean

Dedication

I'd like to thank everyone who has ever believed
in me and has been complimentary about my
work. This book is really dedicated to you.

LEAD ME TO THE WEIRD PLACES

A Hermit's Book of Madness

Joel Dean

Quantum
Dot
Press

To JOHN, I hope You ENJOY. FROM JOEl

Copyright © 2023 Joel Dean.

All rights reserved. No part of this publication may be
reproduced, distributed, or transmitted in any form or by any
means, including photocopying, recording, or other
electronic or mechanical methods, without the prior written
permission of the author, except in the case of brief
quotations embodied in critical reviews and certain other
noncommercial uses permitted by copyright law.

ISBN: 978-1-912882-70-0

Places are used fictitiously. Names, characters, and places
are products of the author's imagination.

Front cover image by LightSpeedDreams.net
Book design by Quantum Dot Press.

Acknowledgements

Thanks to Edwin Rydberg for his work in bringing the book to publication and designing the cover.

Thanks also to Ceri Wilkins, whose photographs of the Hermit were used in the creation of the book cover and as the accompanying image to Who is the Man Behind this Mystery? Ceri's website is: www.rainbowricephotography.com.

Finally, my thanks to Matt Wyatt for his proof-reading, creative suggestions and his continued support and encouragement.

A Note About the Deluxe Service*

If simply buying this book is not a weird enough experience for you, perhaps you would like to consider the deluxe service. George Perkins will dress up as an angel and visit you in the middle of the night. He will then recite the poem Lead Me to the Weird Places as if it were an enchantment. He will take you by the hand and lead you to the Hermit's gravestone. He will give you a shovel and command you to dig. You will not find the Hermit's bones, for at the time of writing he is still very much alive, as far as he can tell, all things considered, and his limbs are still firmly attached. However, what you will discover is the book. Then you can have a picture taken with George, take the book home with you and read it or alternatively go back to sleep or alternatively you can have breakfast early. It really is up to you.

*Offer is only available during dreams or nightmares and may or may not be remembered.

Disclaimer

Some works included within this Hermit's Book of Madness may depict disturbing images or ideas. If this surprises or upsets you… what else did you expect to find in a book of madness?

Nevertheless, please consider carefully whether you'd like to continue. In no way should you dwell too long on the madness within nor attempt to emulate thoughts or deeds discussed or described.

You have been warned and neither the Hermit nor his publisher take any responsibility for the effects upon your mental health should you continue to read beyond this point.

Forward

It is the Hermit of Harrogate's will that this book be published. My name is George Perkins, and I am here to proclaim his will. He chose me because I am mad, and the Hermit of Harrogate looks very favourably on those that are mad.

I met him in a pub one day eating a scotch egg and a curry at the same time, a miraculous act if ever there was one. He said that he was a bit bored of his life and wanted to be worshiped as a god. He asked me whether I would like to be his prophet. I replied in the affirmative. He then said if I am to be worshipped then the people must know my words. If I tell them to you, will you write them down for me? You know, act as my scribe?

As the world was spinning far too fast for me, I agreed. I thought it would slow things down a bit.

The book you now hold in your hands is the result. If you enjoy this book and would like to worship the Hermit, then do please let me know, and I will pass it onto him as best as I can.

There is a part of me that would like to rise above the Hermit and become a god myself, but I know this is wickedness talking and I mustn't give into it. It would make the Hermit angry and spoil our relationship, not to mention ruin our daytrips to Scarborough. Besides there is nothing mystical about the name George Perkins. It is far too sensible and commonplace.

I wish the Hermit's origin story and how I met him were a bit more dramatic, but it is exactly how I describe. Perhaps you could come up with a more exciting mythology. I have tried to myself and failed miserably.

I think what we'd like to make clear is that both of us are not trying to deceive you, we're not saying the things in this book really happened, but they might have happened and that is enough for us. Hopefully it will be enough for you too.

Anyway, I hope you enjoy the book, take it to heart and become a convert a bit like me.

From the Hermit of Harrogate's loyal scribe and proclaimer of his will,

George Perkins
(Also, part time lavatory attendant.)

Introduction

Hello. I'm The Hermit of Harrogate but you've probably gathered that by now and it's nice to gather things from time to time on occasion, occasionally.

So here we are all assembled in the jolly old introduction. Isn't it spooky? Doesn't it remind you of an enchanted manuscript, with all the magic words that thrill and beguile and make you think that life is not so bad after all?

I have authored this book to be deeply boring for that has been my one great aspiration in life. I've never had an interest in being interesting. Such a thing bores me. I long for rainy days, empty bus shelters and people dribbling incontinently in untidy corridors.

I have also authored this book to be stranger than I am because I do not feel I am strange enough already. There's always room for improvement, as they say.

Perhaps this book is one great big magic spell. Perhaps it is just a figment of an overactive imagination. Perhaps it is just a madman's dream on a hot sunny day in the asylum. Perhaps these words will run away once they've been read never to be seen again. Who can tell?

But I want to show you things, reveal things, leave things behind. The universe is full of hidden strangeness, and I want to reveal it all through my writing. Whether I have succeeded, even to a small degree, I leave for my readers to judge. Life is always a complex thing.

All proceeds of this book will go towards setting me up in my ideal permanent base- a cottage in the centre of a hedge maze. Then people can visit me and tell me all sorts of fantastical tales and I can collect them in a massive tome. We will be a most convivial consortium.

Think of this book as a blood-spattered diary plucked from the arms of a ravaged corpse. I offer it as a means of escape, as a gateway to paradise or, at the very least, a daytrip to Scarborough.

I need to get this book out there, because I need something that reflects my personal experience. Perhaps these stories and poems will chime with you. I can only hope that they do, for it will save me from the dark abyss.

For there will always be truth somewhere, there will always be acceptance, beauty, and tolerance. You must go and search for them. Perhaps you will find them here, where the wild things dwell.

Set out on this journey with me and you will see such sights as you never dreamed of. You will discover things that will make you go mad. You will behold the terrors that haunt my soul. For there is murder somewhere. There is death but perhaps the power of my words will heal you or at the very least give you something to think about as you wait in the dark.

I would have written more but being a hermit, I'm not supposed to compose at all, but I've done this on the sly while the master was at his gin and his mistress and his Monopoly. He is quite a busy man. I mean I know you desperately wanted that new bike for Christmas, but this will have to do.

Anyway, I do hope you continue to enjoy life.

Oh yeah, I also want to be worshiped as a god, but I think Georgie boy's already mentioned that, the daft bugger. If that's something that interests you let him know and he'll let me know and we'll all live happily ever after or something like that.

Farewell for now!

Now that you're
properly prepared...

Let's Begin!

Owing to the fact I'm very strange,
There'll be no buns for tea,
There'll be no glittering chandeliers,
There'll be no monsters lurking.

There'll just be teacakes and cupcakes and
cheesecakes and plum cakes,
There'll be apples and strawberries and jam.
Then we'll marry beneath the whispering forest,
And pretend we've known each other for several
centuries.
Clop.

Have You Seen the Ruins?

I stood there in the half-light. The blood was dripping from my knife. I had killed her. I had killed my tormentor.

It all started two months ago when I moved into my new basement flat. A different town, a fresh start in life or so I thought.

I'll never forget the night it first occurred. I was working on my thriller, set in turn of the century bohemian Paris. I'd reached the point where Jack declared his love for Margaret when all of a sudden, I heard someone trudge, trudge, trudge down the stairs.

I looked up. Who would want me at this time of night? There was a tap at the door.

I don't quite know why but I felt slightly panicky- irrational I know. Perhaps it was because of my weariness or the lateness of the hour. I wondered if I should ignore it. Couldn't it wait until the morning? However, something compelled me to open the door.

I was greeted by the sight of a dear, sweet old lady. She was about five foot two and wore a grey jacket and skirt. Although there can be no denying the sweetness in her features there was also something disturbingly menacing about her. Maybe it was the way she stared at me. She was looking through me, gazing past me, a dead expression on her face. Eventually I spoke.

"Can… can I help you?" I stumbled.

"Have you seen the ruins?" She responded.

"Ruins- what ruins?" I enquired.

Yet the old lady spoke not a word more. She simply turned and trudged, trudged, trudged back up the stairs.

I was perturbed. What on Earth was the old bat doing, disturbing people in the middle of the night, asking potty questions? What could she mean by the ruins?

The next day I tried to concentrate on crafting my masterpiece, but the mysterious occurrence kept preying on my mind. I tried going for a walk, but it did little good. So, by evening an early night seemed my only course of action.

I just couldn't get to sleep that night. I tossed and turned. I felt strangled somehow. Then I sat up drenched in sweat. For I heard the same trudge, trudge, trudge as the night before. The tap on the door came again and reluctantly I got out of bed. I opened the door and there was my visitor from the previous night.

"Do you want a cup of tea?" I queried, trying desperately to sound friendly.

But all she voiced was her demented inquiry in that scratchy, squeaky voice of hers. Then she trudged, trudged, trudged back up the stairs leaving me confused and alone.

This happened every single night. I have absolutely no doubt that she did it even when I was visiting friends. Once when I was spending the night with Nigel Barrington, an old friend and fellow writer, a postcard was found amongst his other correspondence. Completely baffled he handed it to me. I read with disgust the words "have you seen the ruins." In a fit of rage, I tore it up and flung it into Nigel's fire. I was a poor companion to Nigel from that moment on.

One night, she did her usual routine then out of sheer desperation, I dropped to my knees, grabbed hold of her and beseeched.

"Look what ruins? Please I don't understand and believe me I want to understand. They're obviously important else why would you call on me each night? Just please, please tell me more."

Yet despite my entreaties as usual she said nothing and trudged, trudged, trudged back up the stairs.

As I knelt there weeping, despairing, the idea formed in my mind. I would kill the old woman.

That is exactly what I did the subsequent night. No scream came from her, she merely slumped to the floor, as if a puppeteer had cut her strings. She lay on the ground and groggily I went to bed. I'd deal with it in the morning.

Yet instead of the peace I expected, I was

plagued by terrible nightmares- visions of people burning in scorching Hell, horrific demons inflicting pain and an endless stream of blood.

I mechanically got out of bed. The old woman's body had vanished. I went through the front door and outside there was nought but rubble, wreckage, and destruction. Civilization had been utterly annihilated. I had no idea what had happened, but I had finally seen them. I had finally seen the ruins.

The Man Who Had No Money

Once upon a time there was a man who decided to telephone the police because he had no money.

"Excuse me, I wondered if you could help me, only I've got no money you see, and I need some to pay my electricity bill."

"Well, I'm very sorry to hear that sir. The trouble is I'm quite hard up myself at the moment, but I'll tell you what I'll do. I'll tell you a story."

"A story? What good will that do? I need cash fast!"

"You see, I was in my local the other day minding my own business. As a matter of fact, I was devouring a packet of nuts. Well, I say nuts, it was more a bag of salt and vinegar crisps. I digress. Suddenly the door creaked open and in came this very bizarre looking man with a great sprawling black beard right down to his middle. He was about six foot seven and moaned and groaned and dribbled all down his matted whiskers. He didn't so much walk as shuffle desperately; his legs spread absurdly wide, making huge efforts to drag his cumbersome feet. The reason for his eccentric gait was an indissoluble mystery to me and I looked at him in complete and utter bewilderment."

6

"Slowly, dreadfully he lumbered towards me, this great hulking beast of a peasant. He came to an abrupt halt by bumping carelessly into my table. He let out an enormous wail of pain. When he reached the end of his mournful dirge, he pointed a horrible, foul finger at me and declared in a repugnant voice that seemed to emanate from the bowels of Hell:

"In my possession, I have a map leading to the lost treasure of Captain Roger Tuppence. Would you care to own it?"

I didn't really know what to say. It was such a strange proposition. I hesitated and stuttered, beads of perspiration dripping from my brow, such was the sense of unease the peculiar creature inspired within me. But the uncompromising monster did not suffer my dillydallying lightly.

"Answer me now, you silly old fool, or I'll start spitting left, right and centre."

"Ok. Ok. I'll take your dratted map just please don't hurt me."

"The peculiar creature produced a crumpled piece of paper from his pocket, chucked it at me indignantly and it landed in my soup which was odd because I hadn't really ordered soup, just a loaf of nonsense."

"The peculiar creature turned, moaned a sad farewell, and shuffled in his unusual manner slowly out of the door. I sat there relieved at having survived the dreadful ordeal and muttered several thanks to my lord Jesus Christ with my eyes turned skyward."

"I have kept the chart from that day to this, not knowing what to do with it or even where to put it. Quite frankly I look on it more as a burden than a blessing, so you are welcome to it if it is any use to you whatsoever."

There was a pause as the man on the other end of the telephone digested this weird tale.

"Sir?" The policeman prompted after several seconds of silence.

"Send it round."

With that the man who had no money abruptly hung up.

After ringing back with his address which he forgot to mention, the man who had no money sat in silence for several days eagerly awaiting the arrival of the treasure map and hoping the final demand for his electricity bill would not turn up first. His mouth watered at the prospect of becoming immensely rich.

Then came the day the map dropped onto his mat. When he heard it land, he stopped everything, ran to his front door, and quickly tore open the envelope. Of course, he didn't know it was the map, but he had a feeling in his bones and that was good enough for him. He unfolded the contents of the packet and beheld the treasure map in all its glory. A wide grin spread across his funny little face.

The map told him that the fortune lay somewhere in South Africa so without a moment's delay the man who had no money put on his trilby and raincoat and went outside to a bright sunny day. He wasn't completely sure where South Africa was, but he felt that if he kept walking, he'd come across it eventually.

The man who had no money had perambulated barely a few metres when he found himself falling down a hole he had not spotted, so intent was he on studying his map. It was not altogether an unpleasant experience tumbling down this chasm, in a way it felt quite liberating, but the fact was it distinctly ran against his original intention of walking to South Africa, discovering the treasure and paying his electricity bill. As he plummeted, he contemplated the whole business of this strange venture and felt a profound sense of the absurdity and pointlessness of existence.

From his vantage point behind some bushes, the shuffling, dribbling man with the great sprawling black beard viewed the nasty, queer accident with undisguised mirth. He then produced a shovel and promptly filled in the hole.

This completed the peculiar, shuffling, dribbling man headed in the direction of the nearest public house with a fresh Captain Roger Tuppence treasure map in his pocket to start the whole sorry chain of events all over again. He wouldn't miss the treasure map as he had hundreds more at home.

The moral of this story, if story it may be, is beware peculiar, shuffling, dribbling men who give you treasure maps. They may have hundreds more at home.

King of Magic

Today I told the job centre man life is strange. He agreed with me to an extent. He said it can be. After the conversation had ended, I said to Mam that was the scariest thing I've ever done and laughed hysterically. I don't know whether to view this as a victory or a defeat. Maybe it's a little of both. You see, I like to bamboozle people with nonsense. It's my stock in trade. It's what the King of Magic would do, and he is my god. He's the reason you see grinning faces in clouds. He's the reason tables sometimes fly around the room apparently at random. He's the reason why mice scream at shadows. He's the reason clocks aren't mirrors and vice versa. He's the reason toenail clippings disappear on Sundays. He's the reason trains get eaten up by railway tunnels. He is the inspiration for all your nursery rhymes and the answer to all your riddles.

I have been searching for the King of Magic and if you look for something hard enough, you will find it. I rather fear when I do encounter this figure, it will be my doppelganger, and he will lead me, Pied Piper like, to that dark cave from which there is no return and there will be several people, beckoning me to safety from their bright, welcoming homes but the King of Magic's enchantments will prove too strong, and I will not be able to resist his mesmeric power. There is a darkness in this world which we cannot fight. It is for those left behind to keep the candles burning. Perhaps they will have more success next time. Emily implored Bagpuss to be golden and light. I would beg the same of the King of Magic and for the cave to be full of glittering delights. I'm not sure I will be so lucky.

Today I met the King of Magic for the first time in forever. I asked him where he had been. He told me he had been supping wine amongst the dead and generally making a nuisance of himself. I congratulated him on his bizarre activities and shared my sincere hope to encounter him on a more regular basis. His response to that was both cruel and mystifying. He spat hot chestnuts in my face.

Salvation

I had been wandering in the forest I know not how long. Sometimes it felt like a few seconds. Sometimes an eternity. Time was meaningless to me. It had turned to ashes along with everything else in this stupid world and yet somehow, I had resisted the urge to end it all. Instead, I had decided to take refuge in the forest.

Why was I doing this? What could I be hoping to achieve? Was I trying to get into the spirit of nature, embrace the Green Man, cavort with the fairies? I don't know. Perhaps it was a simple quest to find peace. I wanted to reject the world. I wanted to turn my back on the life I had lived up to this point. The things I had seen. All of it so needless, so pointless, so pitiful. Yet there was the constant nagging doubt that I was just being foolish, that I should stop being silly and return home to my responsibilities but frankly I couldn't be bothered.

The darkness was crowding in now reflecting I fancied the blackness raging in my soul. The forest wasn't comforting at all. I was cold, wet, hungry, and tired. My tattered uniform was caked in mud and all I could see in the darkness were terrible, mournful things. I was searching for some justification in what I was doing. It was then that I saw a light flickering in the darkness.

As I drew nearer and my eyes became accustomed, I saw that it was the luminescence of a campfire, the wood crackling as it burnt. On a log sat a very tired looking old man. His back hunched in despair, his long unwashed white hair straggling messily down to his shoulders. He looked more like a decaying husk than anything else. After watching him for a few minutes in which he sat as still as a rock I stepped boldly forward.

To my surprise the old man did not flinch, did not cry out in alarm, for I had appeared unannounced and as we were quite deep in the forest, I imagined he did not get many wayfarers. I supposed he might take me for a brigand, and it would be my job to assuage his fears. But he merely looked up at me with a smile stretched across his wrinkled face. It felt almost as if he had been expecting me.

"Welcome friend. Please make yourself comfortable."

He gestured with his bony, frail arm to another log by the fire, directly opposite to where he was sitting. Dumbly I obeyed, for my mind was too tired to question whether I could trust this man.

"Tell me. What brings you to this part of the forest?" he asked. His voice was gentle, kind and inspired me to confess all.

"I am lost."

"Lost?"

He looked at me as if genuinely concerned, as if he understood the pain that such a feeling could cause.

"Not lost in the forest. Lost in life. Though I suppose I am lost in the physical sense as well. I don't know. I hadn't really thought about it. I suppose to be truly lost one must have a destination in mind.

I suppose I did not have an awareness of one."

The old man looked thoughtful. "Perhaps I might be your ultimate destination. Or at least what I represent."

"And what is that?"

"A simple life of duty, service and devotion to God."

At this he began to stoke the fire with a fork. He then produced a plate of vegetable stew from under his raggedy cloak and offered it to me. I was confused. I could see steam rising from it and the smell was mouth-watering to my rumbling stomach but there was no evidence of him having prepared it. Though strange I was too hungry to worry about it.

The food was beautiful. It filled my belly as I ravenously gulped it down. Every mouthful brought warmth and cheer back within me. I noticed he was not eating and wondered why. Perhaps he had eaten earlier. Then again, he looked like he hadn't eaten in months, almost to the point of starvation. He watched me all the time I was guzzling greedily and to my imagination assumed the aspect of a sinister glaring witch fattening up a child, ready to peel off my skin and place me in a boiling cauldron. Perhaps it was just my idle fancy or the way the dancing fire cast its shadows.

"Are you not eating" I enquired, wishing to break the uncomfortable silence.

The old man smiled weakly.

"I try to keep my appetite in check."

I did not know quite what he meant by this. Perhaps he was trying to avoid the sin of gluttony.

"So, what brings you to this life of solitude and devotion to God? I take it you would call yourself a hermit?"

"Yes, I suppose so. I am a sinner. A weak and miserable sinner. I knew that I could not be around people without corrupting them, harming them, leading them onto the path of wickedness and so I came out here. To seek solitude. To seek salvation. To try and curb my sinful ways."

He looked away from the fire and held me in his inscrutable gaze. I was surprised to discover that his eyes were wet with tears.

"I am glad you have come. I have had no company for many a week. Perhaps you are my salvation. And yet... and yet I am afraid."

I felt a great sympathy for this old hermit.

There seemed to be an incurable sadness haunting and cursing his soul. I did not know what I could do to help. I felt powerless. Seeing my troubled expression, the hermit stood up.

"And now you have filled your belly you must rest. For sleep is the only peace some of us can find. Either that or death. For some of us, at least."

He picked up a lantern and led me into a small cave. Although not the most congenial accommodation it was blissful shelter and I felt safe here, like I was entering a protective womb, in which Mother Nature would bless and comfort me.

"I offer you my sanctuary, for you will not be able to find your way back tonight. Once you are in the forest it consumes you. She does not let her children leave easily. Well goodnight."

The hermit blew out the lantern pitching the cave in total darkness. I had not lain down to sleep yet, so I clumsily lowered myself to the floor. Sleep did not come speedily, and thoughts drifted around my mind.

I would like to say that this hermit had deeply impressed me. That I felt drawn to the simplicity of his life. That this was the path I had been searching for. That I was excited by the new life he had presented to me, but the truth is more complex than that. All that it is accurate to say is that I did feel like I wanted to stay and help this man if I could.

Then I heard faint sobbing that swiftly

transformed into the most pitiful clamorous wailing imaginable. Then the most lamentable cry of:

"Oh God, oh God. Please forgive me!"

The wailing continued until it had burnt itself out. I tried to shut out the sorrow. It affected my own heart to hear it. It had risen a little since the food, warmth and shelter and I desperately didn't want it to sink again. Perhaps I should bring this man away with me, find some role in society he would be comfortable with. Whatever this sin was that he referred to was evidently causing him a great deal of distress. Perhaps I could help him get over it whatever it was. It could be anything. Perhaps it was murder. Perhaps he was a remorseful fugitive of the law. That might be it. If so, he wasn't so very different from me. Perhaps we could help each other.

The sorrow bred terrible nightmares. First, I saw the Hermit somewhere up in the night sky laughing manically, his face contorted in hideous demented merriment. I saw myself in the bubbling cauldron that my idle fancy had conjured up earlier in the evening. Finally, and most vividly of all I saw the hermit wandering in the forest. Slowly the ancient trees began to twist into a new shape, that of crosses dripping with red wine. The hermit skipped and cavorted madly around them as if they were maypoles and drank deeply the libation, until he was quite intoxicated and fell stupidly into a ditch. A withered priest shambled in and coughed and spluttered his way through the burial service as he threw earth on the hermit's body, but I could tell he was not truly dead, for it horribly twisted and writhed throughout.

I sat up suddenly with beautiful warm light all around me and happily I embraced the morning. It was a wonderful feeling after the cold, dark and confusion of the night and all the wicked dreams that had plagued me. I enjoyed the peace of waking. Then I noticed the hermit had gone.

Groggily and stiffly, I walked out of the cave into the brightness of the morning and the singing birds. He was nowhere to be seen. I pondered my next course of action when I heard the distinct sound of noisy slurping. It was a gross and uncivilised sound, like that of an animal. Curiously, I followed the noise with the sound growing louder and somehow more disturbing by the second until at last it guided me to a little clearing.

There I stood aghast. A horribly mutilated carcass of a deer lay before my eyes. It looked as if it had been savagely ripped apart with superhuman strength. It was a desecration of the sanctity of nature but not as bad as the other desecration that met my eyes. The hermit was hovering over this poor creature, his mouth pressed to its oozing wounds. As the hermit sucked the blood it somehow fell through him and splattered nosily onto the floor, forming a hideous pool. Slowly he stopped as if sensing my presence and his body fell to the ground. He looked up. His eyes briefly gave way from animal ferocity back to the pitiful ones of the old man I had known the night before.

"I tried. Really, I did. My God, he will not say that I did not try. Three days dead, just like Christ. He said turn away from your sins and you will live again. The old man tilted his head back and laughed, a repulsive, iniquitous, deranged, old cackle that poisoned the whole forest with its wretched blasphemy.

"Live again." The hermit sneered. Then he yelled with the utmost savage aggression "what did He mean "'live again?'" This isn't raindrops on my skin. This isn't the sweet smell of flowers. This isn't the joys of the forest. This is emptiness. A stabbing, kicking, screaming emptiness. No beginning, no middle, no end. Just waves of deafening silence crashing on the shore. And yet this thirst. The one scrap thrown to me without care, like the lords at the high table to the wretched mongrels. And what good will it do me? It will not stay inside. It will not restore me to flesh. Why would He do this? Where is His mercy? Where is His love? Or was I beyond all that a long time ago? Is this my Hell? A useless lust that will not leave me?"

Swiftly he floated towards me. His form seemed to separate like a mist, and I felt trapped on every side. Suddenly a mighty wind began billowing recklessly, stripping the trees of their luscious greenery. The temperature plummeted to that of the depths of icy winter. All I could see was the hermit's old face full of malevolence in front of me. It began laughing and screaming until my ears burst and I could hear no more. Then I experienced the worst pain of all. I felt my neck cleanly twisted to his impish will, a vice-like grip around my throat as life escaped me.

I could not say why I ventured into the forest. I was not sure what I had been seeking. I realised now it was salvation and the same was true of the old hermit. As I felt the last stains of existence leave me, I could not tell which one of us would receive it. All I could do was just accept and settle myself down for a long and perhaps eternal sleep. For sleep is the only peace some of us can find. Either that or death. For some of us at least. I prayed that I had been good.

Follow the Prophet

Josiah Smedley sat back in his comfortable red leather armchair and emitted a loud contented sigh. The meeting had gone well. The collective faith of all the people had been truly inspiring. What's more, he felt like he was achieving his dream of uniting mankind through common belief which was a noble thing in his view. Perhaps along the way he had been a little dishonest, but he thought he could live with that. It was a small price to pay for the good he felt he was doing.

As he sat there, he began to ponder the future of the church after he was gone. He ought to give some consideration to that. No use dying unexpectedly and everything going up in the air, leaving people in confusion and uncertainty.

Just then, there was a knock at the door and in walked what can only be described as a complete and utter mystery.

The figure wore a raincoat, trilby and plimsoles, all in a cosmic, hypnotic black. In addition, Stygian tights clung to his spindly insect legs. Where his face would've been there was nothing but darkness, yet if you looked closely, you could just make out a bump where his nose might have been. How was this effect achieved? Surely it must be some kind of mask without holes for eyes or mouth, but Josiah could not be certain.

"Who are you? What do you want? How did you get in here?" The flood of questions spouted swiftly and loudly from Josiah's mouth.

"I, sir, am God, which is to say I am a mystery, for who of us can actually say we have seen God or even heard his voice?"

"I have, sir, for I am a prophet. You see I had the inspiration to seek him out in faith because I lacked wisdom and God spoke to me. He spoke to me because it was his time to speak. He told me that none of the churches were true and that I must restore his gospel in the latter days."

"Lies! Balderdash! Piffle!" Screamed the stranger, his hot rage bubbling over like a witch's cauldron. "You, sir, are nothing but a hoodwinker and a charlatan. A conniver! An imposter! A fraud! I will not tolerate your cruel deceptions any longer. I challenge you to a duel."

With this, the stranger slapped the prophet with a pair of white kid gloves he produced from his raincoat pocket. The prophet drew in his breath sharply at such a vulgar display of barbarous brutality.

"Sir, I accept your outrageous challenge. It is clear to me that you are not our beloved saviour at all but probably a poor lunatic escaped from some asylum or other, no doubt unhinged with insane delusions. In any case, whoever you are, the devil has got inside you. You are an emissary of Satan, and I will stamp out your wickedness if it's the last thing I do."

"You will meet me outside the city jail in precisely one hour. The duel will be with pistols. Until then, I do not want you to read scriptures and pray in an attempt to try and increase your spiritual strength. No sir, I wish you to suffer horribly in a diabolical agony. I want your soul to mourn at the hell that is awaiting you. For it will be a special kind of Hades that awaits. A coldness, a blankness, a nothingness. Think of this as the final hour before your execution. I bid you good day, you stupid old fool!"

Before the prophet could strike him in anger, the stranger disappeared in a puff of black, billowing smoke. The prophet coughed and spluttered. He ran to the window and opened it, gulping down delicious breaths of fresh air. The icy blast froze his skin. A snowy blizzard was raging outside. As the room cleared, he tried to do the same with his muddled head. Who was that man? Was he an agent of the devil? Was this some kind of test of his faith? Or had this demon come to punish him for spreading lies? The prophet's intent had always been good. He meant no harm in his actions.

Then suddenly the answer became clear, like a

mighty galleon emerging from a cloying mist. For he suddenly realised this was his way to become a martyr. This was the means that would guarantee his religion would endure. Give the people a martyr. Give them someone who dies for the things he believes in, and people would propagate his message for generations to come. Statues would be erected, millions of converts baptised, temples and churches would dot the globe. Millions shall know Brother Josiah again.

"Wiggins!"

"Yes, Mr. Smedley?"

"Rally the people. It is time for our final meeting."

"Final, sir? Why? Where is you goin'?"

"Oh, just a little place called Heaven. I don't know if you've heard of it. But don't worry. I will not only have life everlasting, but I will sit with the saints among the elite."

"Why, sir? Is you dying or somethin'?"

The prophet looked at the face of this odious, deformed peasant and felt something akin to the love a mother has for her imperfect son. For those blessed eyes see nought but perfection though the world beyond judges and cackles impiously. The prophet kissed tenderly Wiggins' bulbous, ruddy nose and lapped up the stray mucus with his solicitous tongue.

"All shall be revealed in good time. But first-the people!"

"Yes sir!"

Wiggins gave an overenthusiastic salute and hit himself in the face. He then pulled up his trousers and ran to the city square, all the while blowing a trumpet tunelessly and ringing a bell.

"Wake up, you bastards" he screamed idiotically. "The prophet has called another meeting!"

Wiggins punched in doors, broke windows with stones and defecated on nicely trimmed lawns in his wild ebullience. He would probably have to write several letters of apology in the morning, but it would all be worth it for he was doing the prophet's work.

"Why the fuck is Wiggins calling another meeting? The barmy bastard! I think he must be mentally ill or something."

"Ooh I don't know, dear. Perhaps it is a test of faith- to see if we will not only go to regular meetings but also to ones called spontaneously."

"But it is a very late hour and I have to be up for work tomorrow."

"God will bless your righteousness, dearest love." And after a gentle kiss the couple set off for the meeting house.

When they arrived, it was packed. Wiggins was playing the organ beautifully, filing the air with sweet music. There was general hubbub; people wondering what was going on. Then Wiggins leaped up and banged his gavel on the head of one of the members of the congregation.

"Order in the court! Order in the court!"

"I'll have a pastrami on rye" said a passing squirrel, in a scurrilous attempt to be thoroughly cheeky.

"Really Squirrel! This isn't a cafe! This is a house of God! How many more times do I have to tell you?"

"Sorry, sir."

The passing squirrel was so mortified at this rebuke that he immediately went into the vestry to cut his own head off. Giuseppe continued.

"Ladies and gentlemen, your friend and mine, jolly Jack prophet!"

A large round of applause, cheers and whistles greeted the Prophet's entrance.

"Really Giuseppe! This isn't a music hall. This is a house of God. How many more times do I have to tell you?

"Sorry, sir."

Giuseppe Wiggins was so mortified at *this* rebuke that he too immediately went into the vestry to cut his own head off because they do say that two heads are better than one.

The prophet looked out at his loving congregation and had a moment's pause, held still by their pleading eyes, like lost little lambs. He was their shepherd and he had gathered them all up. The prophet knew that his news would be quite a rotten cabbage for them to digest but felt it was essential for the ongoing journey of his message. Who knows where that glorious journey could end? Nonetheless he could not help but be moved by the unity of faith he had inspired within them. Close to tears, he began.

"My friends, thank you so much for coming. I gathered you all here because... well there's no easy way of saying this... but... I am going to my death."

There were sharp intakes of breath as well as a few "no not thats" and "I say, steady ons," shocked as they were by this terrible announcement.

"My friends, please. I want to reassure you that everything will be alright. This church will go on without me. In this envelope I have a divine revelation of what must happen next which I shall give to Giuseppe Wiggins before I go. I would like you all to know that I do not fear death. On the contrary, I'm rather looking forward to it. I've packed my bucket and spade and everything and if this is my destiny, well, so be it. We will now sing the closing hymn."

"But Josiah, what do you mean you are going to your death?" asked an old man. "Who is it that means you ill? Surely, we could all rally round and protect you."

"Oh Peter, before this evening is out, you will

deny me three times."

"My name isn't Peter, it's Nigel."

"Oh, that's alright then. The Bible doesn't say anything about Nigels. Or the revelation in this envelope for that matter."

"I've got a mate called Judas if that's any help."

"No, it really isn't!" replied the prophet, slightly annoyed but trying to smile politely.

"Goodbye my friends!"

The prophet went through the congregation shaking people's hands. It really was a piteous site. People were wailing. pulling their hair out, gnashing their teeth. One woman, in her blind rage, started smashing up the organ with an axe. It didn't really matter as the closing hymn was soon forgotten about anyway as the prophet put on his winter cloak and strode out bravely into the swirling snow.

Outside the city jail, the prophet began to hear drumbeats but there was no sign of that percussion instrument anywhere. He knew he was being marched to his death. The mysterious stranger was stood on a platform, but he wasn't waiting for a train. He was waiting for this beautiful moment. The stranger laughed manically, his evil cackle drowning out the sound of the howling wind.

"So, Josiah, come to die, have we?"

"To accept my fate, certainly."

"Very well, so be it."

The stranger leapt off the platform like a demonic jack in the box, his claw like hands instantly grabbing and squeezing the prophet's throat. His demented laughing rang horribly in his ear and then the stranger started screaming.

"I am God! I am God! I am God! This is the last thing you will ever know. That I am God, and this is my everlasting power. My will. To decide. Who lives, who dies. Who wins, who loses. And you will die just like that god you profess to worship."

With that, the stranger tore off the prophet's clothes and shoved him to the ground. With the utmost horror, the prophet beheld a cross lying there. The stranger laid him out upon it and began hammering nails into his fingers. The spurting blood gave the stranger immense erotic pleasure and he actually ejaculated all over the prophet's body.

The cross was hauled up as if by magic and the stranger contemplated his handiwork with relish. He had created art from violent execution. He had routed his first false prophet and he was on his way to creating the world in his own image.

The stranger took out a notebook and crossed off Josiah Smedley off his list. Thanks to him, millions will never know Brother Josiah again.

He then produced his camera phone and a ladder, took a selfie with the horrible, bloody corpse, and uploaded it onto social media. This completed, he calmly climbed down, put away his instrument of death and vanished into the night.

When the townsfolk discovered the grisly spectacle on the morrow, they felt a deep sickness. Despite the prophet's hopes, his church soon disbanded. If belief bred such horror, the people thought, then perhaps they were better off without it.

And the one man who could have avenged Josiah was dead. Giuseppe Wiggins lay in a pool of his own blood and a cat had started nibbling at his festering brain. You see, it needed a dessert after the squirrel.

Empty Milk Bottles

I met a man the other day who refused to live. He just sort of sat there in his corner declining even to move. He breathed in and out, slowly, and dreadfully and I grew to despise him. I thought he was a total bastard. So, I thought, within this situation, there are two things I could potentially do. I could try and love him, bring him chocolates and flowers, garland him with my sweetest thoughts. Or I could kill him.

I weighed up the two options. I thought black is black and red is red. So I decided to kill him. Can't remember how I did it exactly. It's all a bit of a blur. I think I lost track of time. I remember some mice running away and I thought "ah, the animals know, they are wise."

So, after that I sort of buried his body in a bit of scrubland I know because I often pass it at night, never during the day, though. I don't go out during the day. And that was that I thought. I had rid myself. I was free to do as I chose. I could visit the sweetshop. I could see things more clearly. I could breathe more.

However, I didn't end up doing any of those things because I hadn't really managed to get rid of the man. The spirit of him possessed me and it made me troubled, sad. He threw metaphorical biscuits at me in a taunting manner. If only I'd learnt to live properly, I'd be happier now, the kingdom would be mine. I would see things more clearly than I had ever seen them before. I would understand things people could only imagine and I would be silent. Happy and silent.

Then I thought perhaps it is not the spirit of the old man. Perhaps it is God that is punishing me for my wickedness. For I am a very naughty man. Life is death to me. So it is. It is so.

I didn't do anything for a good deal of time after that. I tried to pray to God, but it didn't work. I saw some lamps flickering amongst the trees outside and I thought possibly it might be a procession of burly woodman who might be able to assist me in my plight but unfortunately it turned out to be a mirage which irritated me enormously.

Then one day a mighty angel did manage to rescue me. Well, that might not have happened. I'm not sure. I started feeling a bit better, though. Apart from killing that man. I decided to seek him out.

"I'm sorry for killing you" I said.

He didn't say anything. That was the most dreadful thing about it. I'd have understood if he was really angry. I would have sympathised deeply, but he forever remained impassive even in death.

So really all I've been doing is tidying up empty milk bottles. It's not very interesting but it might as well be me. I view at as a sort of penance for killing that man. So, it's bringing me a bit of peace, a bit of comfort. I don't really cope very well with life. I might be a bit poorly, but empty milk bottles tend to keep me going. You see, in a way, those milk bottles contain the spirit of the man. The man who refused to live.

Little Things

I like to collect things.
Little things.
Little things people left behind.
Little sad churches no one visits.
Little hats little girls used to wear playing in the park
Little broken hearts that were never mended.

But I don't mind confessing to you
The little things fill me with terror
Sometimes at night.
For I imagine the dead will rise
To claim back
Their little things.
I don't know what makes me think that.
The creak on the stairs
The wind howling
The knock on the door
When no-one's expected
Little things.

Little Ghosts

We are all little ghosts
Haunting each other's lives.
Encounter someone in a cafe
Offer them a spare ticket to the moon
Stay with them a while
Learn something of their secrets
Then suddenly lose track
As they merge with the crowd
Slipping through your fingers
Quite slipping your mind.

All of us deluding ourselves
With dreams of sunny jubilee Bank Holiday
immortality
When all the time they wait in the dark
Ready to pounce.
Half-forgotten stories
Locked away in a drawer.
Was it all a trick?

Matresscide

A mattress gave birth to me. I emerged mouselike from its loving springs. Then one day I got into a really vicious argument and killed it. It offered no resistance. It did not scream to Heaven. Its pillow guardians did not leap to its aid as it bled feathers. As I held them to my tear-stained face, letting the delicate fringed plumes caress my skin, I realised I had committed matresscide. The pain of it destroyed me.

A Plea for Tolerance

England are going to win the cup,
Because their hopes are no longer a pup,
But a fully grown-up dog,
That won't be lost in the fog,
Of uncertainty.

For we shall beat the Italians,
They're a load of rapscallions-
No, hang on, that isn't very nice,
Like dog poo or cat sick or mouldy old lice.
It's very wrong to call people names,
Like Egbert or Harry or Dickie or James,
Besides it spoils our merry football games.

So, forget about labels like English, Italians, and
Europeans,
Let's all just play together as sexy human beings.

Martyr's Death

The other day I asked a man if he would like a spectacular martyr's death. He said no, he was alright thanks, he would prefer to try and live forever. I looked on him as if he were mad, as if he'd chickened out on the way to Calvary, as if he were an actor who refused to play his part in the final act, preferring instead to return home for his comfy slippers and his beans on toast. Ever since then I have been growing fine apple trees in my orchard to try and console myself and make some sense of it all, but I know it is futile.

The Beast Within

Why should I transform,
Bare my fangs and snarl and spit,
Imagining all the pain I could inflict,
if I do not keep myself in check?

For there is a beast within
Straining at the leash
Hungry for freedom,
Thirsty for blood.

Please stay within.
Do not rip through
And spread your nasty nightmares
Smothering all with your noxious smoke.

Please heal my soul
And fill me with light
Banish my demons
And lead me from night.

Universe of Strangeness

I will build for you a world,
A universe of strangeness.
And once it is finished,
I will find a box to put it in,
But I will deny you the key.

And that will be the great frustration.
The source of all your tears.
A cosmos of bewilderment,
Just beyond the horizon,
So close and yet so far.

For this god is cruel.
Brutal and laughing
At the traps he sets.
And the tricks he pulls.
Beware.

Worship Me

"Why am I here?"

Jessica sat up sharply in panic and looked at the nurse at the end of her bed. She had a kindly face though aged with the anxieties of a lifetime. She did not take her eyes off her knitting, peering over her golden spectacles perched on the end of her nose.

"Everything's fine. No need to worry. You're here because you need someone to watch over you but that's not a problem. We all need someone to watch over us sometime."

This seemed to satisfy Jessica. She nodded, fell back on her pillow, and closed her eyes.

As she lay there, waiting for the comforting oblivion of sleep, she remembered being dragged away, being told that she was ill, that she needed rest. She remembered Doctor Mathers looking at her father and shaking his head solemnly. They moved their lips, but she could not tell what they said. She felt drowsy; all the images came to her in a whirl, crowding in on her mind. But what had she done to receive this treatment?

Again, Jessica sat up sharply in a panic, but this was allayed by a scene of utter calm. There was an empty chair at the foot of the bed where the nurse had been and empty beds all around. The darkness was becoming diluted as light entered through the high windows. There was in that moment the most blissful silence, something she hadn't experienced for quite some time. Her life had been a continuous mess of noise. Life had not existed before, and it probably would not exist again. Or would it?

Just then she heard footsteps, very faint treads. It was someone with bare feet. Jessica's heart quickened. She thought she had heard that tread long ago and had known it forever. Then she saw a faint light come from the corridor. It went up past the ward windows and then to the glass-panelled double doors which suddenly flew open with a crash. She felt a freezing blast of wind against her face as it whistled through the ward. From whence it came she did not know but it seemed to emanate from that awesome figure that paused for a moment. Bellowing organ music filled the air. It was so loud Jessica put her hand to her ears. The figure passed through the doors slowly and solemnly. It held its hands outstretched on either side displaying gaping, bloody wounds. Horrible oozing wells of blood in each finger and yet she longed to drink from them and feel a kind of healing power. It came to a halt at the end of Jessica's bed and turned to look at her. Despite the wonder of it all, there was something dreadful about that stare. The eyes were dead, glazed over. The mouth lolled horribly with dripping drool. The skin had a horrible green tinge as if of mouldering decay. Jessica shuddered at the loathsome horror of it all.

"I am the way, the truth and the light" it intoned in a deep, sepulchral voice.

"What is it that you want?" Jessica asked dumbly.

The figure paused, as if considering its answer. After a few seconds it gave it's reply.

"Worship."

As it intoned the words a thick, black cloud of smoke came billowing from its mouth. It filled the ward and seemed to spread out like the blackest night. Jessica felt enveloped by it, almost suffocated by it. She had no choice to succumb.

The Darkened Room

The darkened room was made of fish and so I ate the fish and became someone who wasn't real. I'm glad I did this because I hated the world and I wanted to live forever. Jesus Christ passed by my doorway and told me I was the wrong person. I said I didn't believe him, and I shot him. I'm glad. I drank his blood and made him cry. It did me the power of good. I then saw his ghost in the garden, and I've been living like that ever since.

I asked this man the other day if he had one hundred pounds and he told me he had a fish by the sea. He ate the fish and told me how much he loved it. I ate some bacon from a packet and told the mouse how much I loved it.

Jesus Christ is dead. I killed him. I shot his mother and now I am incredibly rich. I once ate seventeen pasties and threw up all over the kitchen floor. The dog ate my sick and now I am truly sorry. I hate the world said the king as he shot his mother. I am going to live forever and be the king of words. I'm going to see things more clearly and then I will understand the way of all flesh. For that is the true meaning of genesis, exodus, and rebirth. I killed an old man the other day, I saw his ghost in the factory and now I am eating pork pies for a living. It is not doing me any good, but I hate the world and now my life is dead, and I am made of fish.

Confused Jumble

I saw a dirty old pedlar,
Shuffling down the street,
Flogging flea-bitten monkeys to deluded organ
grinders,
Selling overripe oranges to the starving.
He stopped me in the street,
Wheeling his confused jumble,
Broken clocks,
Decaying furniture,
Mouldy cheese for the mice.

He said "here, do you want some madness?"
I replied, "no thanks, I've got enough already."
The old pedlar frowned.
"So have I. I can't seem to shift it."

Really Long Arms

Pretend you've got really long arms,
Drag them sadly across the floor
As if the world's caved in.

Then perhaps people will take pity,
Offer you joy.
Or maybe they'll call you freaky long arms.
Snap them off like twigs.

If love is the answer
Then so is kindness.
Treating people right.

It's a simple hope.

The Man Who Wrote a Book

I met a man the other day who wrote a book. I don't know why he did this. Maybe he thought it was a good idea. But one way or another it became a bestseller. People kept coming up to him telling him how brilliant he was, how witty and how clever, how his words were perfectly formed. He grew fed up with this. To the point where he tried to kill himself. Then a monster appeared and told him life was OK. And he believed the monster. He started to call it strange names like Harry and Fred. Then after a while, he disappeared down a well and was never seen nor heard of again which is sad really but it's the way things go or, so it's been said by someone or other. I can't remember who exactly. It must have been someone. I just can't remember.

The Man Who Wrote for Television

I met a man the other day who wrote for television. I asked him why he'd done this. He said he didn't want to and that's why he'd done it. He enjoyed doing things he didn't like doing like killing himself or shaving. He ran into a pub the other day and began to see things that weren't there. He described this experience as strange which I semi-agreed with. He was such a weird man this man. He had no face, no eyes, no teeth. I wanted to ask him to marry me, but I thought it wouldn't do any good, so I didn't.

Have You ever Known?

Have you ever known what it's like to kill a man? I have. It wasn't very nice. I probably shouldn't have done it. I ran away into the park and screamed. I asked God what I had done but I did not receive an answer, so I jumped into the sea with some fish and ever since then I've been living forever which I'm not very glad about. I just don't like people. They get on my nerves. I'd like to stick a knife in one of their eyes and tell them to go eat strawberries, but I doubt very highly that I have the confidence to do such a thing. For I am a very timid man.

Barrier of Pain

Smash through the barrier of pain,
And you will live forever,
God smiles brightly,
Their teeth, he shows them,
In violent streams.

If you think my poem mad,
You've spotted the clue,
To the mystery of it all.

The Knife is The Wand

I need the knife
Deep inside
Twisting my guts
Making me flow like wine

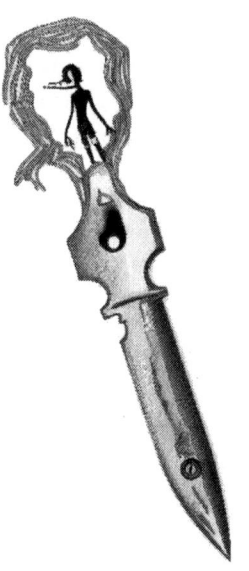

For the knife is the wand
Casting the spell
That will transform.

For the knife is the key
That will unlock
All secrets.

Bury me deep in the earth
Plant me like the seed
From which the flowers grow.

Only then will I be released.
Only then will the egg begin to crack
Only then will the stone roll away
Only then will the sun shine through the storm.

The misery of my life will tyrannise me no longer
It is finished.

25 Menlove Gardens East

I am travelling in a tramcar on my way to 25 Menlove Gardens East. If you would like to know why I am travelling in a tramcar on my way to 25 Menlove Gardens East, it is because I am going to see a man called R M Qualtrough to discuss insurance.

I don't know who this R M Qualtrough is. I have never heard of him before. I do not believe he is a frequenter of fashionable literary salons. Whoever he is, I do not like the sound of him. I think I might kill him if he allows me to do so. If he offers up his heart to my knife.

Because, you know, secretly, I know my journey is a futile one. I know there is no 25 Menlove Gardens East. 25 Menlove Gardens North, South, and West, certainly, but no East, no East. I know that the address is nothing but a stage set, that will be deconstructed when the farce has run its course and that when I stab at Qualtrough, I will be stabbing at a dummy, a scarecrow or worse, my own shadow.

And when I get home, I will find my beautiful wife, lying in a pool of her own blood- the ultimate desecration of life. And I will cry for days but no number of tears will wash away my pain and I feel so powerless about it all, like I have no choice but to play my part, trapped by fate. I feel like I will be getting on tramcars travelling to non-existent addresses meeting malignant fictitious persons for the rest of my life or worse, into eternity. I feel this is my curse, my hell.

And who will save me? When will God descend in his celestial chariot or helicopter, scoop me up and rescue me. Rescue me! How sweet those words! But I know there is no God, just as there is no R M Qualtrough. Perhaps, after all, they are one and the same.

Lost in Madness

Little child
Lost in madness
Have you disappeared in the sea?
Have you become something that isn't you?

If you have then I'll write you a story about champagne.
I'll tell you a wicked tale that has no meaning.
Then perhaps you'll see the truth.
Then again perhaps you won't.
Either way it doesn't really matter.

Great Big Child

If I'm a great big child,
Come and play with me in the zoo,
Or the park or the field or the forest.
Then I can be happy
And put away the pain and fear inside.

For I want to run into the sea
And be a stupid idiot
I want to eat ice creams
And walk to Sandsend.

Maybe then you will love me
And treat me like a child.
If I'm mad, then so are you.

A While Longer

Why don't you dream a while longer
While there's still time
The road is long and weary
And you have grown very old.

I remember you in younger days
When you did not worry so.
And now the dawn is breaking
Letting new life in.

Where is yours now?
What did it become?
Has it reached the point of
breaking?
Will it divide in two?

Oh, if I could but live once
There would be no war,
There would only be fruit
in the bowl,
Handpicked from the tree.

Little Red

So many come here. Some to worship, some to get lost, some to find themselves. I can be a little confusing, but I swear it's not my fault. It's humans that get things mixed up with their muddled little heads. They never learn, do they? Perhaps I should care for them, demonstrate the healing power of nature but I'm just trying to keep it together, you know. People seek what they want to seek here.

I'll never forget Little Red. One day she decided to deliver some food to her sick grandmother and her mother told her to stick to the path.

I don't know if you've ever been on a path. They are something humans create to not get lost. Fancy that! I would argue in my ancient tree-like sort of way that sometimes getting lost is the true path to self-discovery. Actual paths are just the routes to safety. All being well of course. But what if the path were left unfinished? That's a terrifying prospect perhaps one of the most frightening and I haven't even mentioned wolves yet.

You see there are all sorts of creatures lurking in my undergrowth. Stick to the path and you'll be safe. That's what they tell themselves. But we all must confront our demons eventually. Red was only little though. But maybe it's never too early to learn.

One of these creatures was a mighty hungry wolf. There aren't many takeaways in my environs. Little Red coming out of the blue like that. It could tempt the most righteous.

This wolf likes to play games. So, he says "'ere, where do you think you're going?"

So Red tells him. Blabs it all out. That's foolish.

So Wolfie thinks "right- well I've got a brilliant game. I'll go eat her grandma. 'Cos there's nowt like a mature wine and I'm sure she's a very good vintage. But I need a distraction. Ah!"

"Why not pick some flowers? Your grandmother will think it's a lovely thought and then you can tell people a wolf gave you that thought. Then you'll raise our profile somewhat. People won't think we're total bastards."

So Red picks the flowers. People take mementos all the time. Bringing the outside in. Like mud on your boots or Christmas trees. It's nice.

So anyway, Wolfie eats Grandma. Then he thinks "I know. I'll wear some of my meal's clothes. I will become one with the character of my dinner, a bit like that actor who drank some of Genghis Kahn's blood when playing the Mongol Emperor."

Wolfie liked dressing up as Grandma so much he thought this could be his new life. He didn't mind if Red didn't turn up. He probably could skip dessert.

But Red did turn up. So, she brought it on

herself, Wolfie thought. She had sealed her own fate. Suffice it to say Red got eaten and like any good glutton, Wolfie realised there was *always* room for dessert.

This is where our heroic woodcutter comes in. I told him to get over to Red's Grandma's double quick. "Chop, chop" I said. Ha, ha, ha!

He finds Wolfie all full and asleep. He cuts open the beast and removes Granny and Red, like someone having their appendix out and says, "go on, have some stones instead."

This causes Wolfie to waken because putting sones in your stomach isn't a particularly sleepy thing to do like putting on your pyjamas or lying down or indeed eating grandmothers and their grandchildren.

Wolfie tries to flee but doesn't get very far. Stones you see. Quite heavy things. So he collapses and in collapsing perishes. So endeth wolves- for now. But there are plenty more where he came from. Believe me. I know. I hear their howls at night.

Lead Me to the Weird Places

Lead me to the weird places
Let me wander far from the path
Let me slip from your hand
And grasp onto another.

Let me ramble aimlessly
Through cornfields and meadows
Hills and forests
Blindfolded.

I will see the skulls
Embrace death
And live again
Born anew
Through the joy of love.

And who will I see there?
Who will come to greet me?
It will be a stranger
Nothing but a shadow
Black as raven's wing.

But perhaps they will lead me
To the weird places.

A Conclusion, if You Need One

It begins with a love of theatricality. It begins with imagination and what if. It begins with performance and writing and acting and changing the world like everyone else. That's how it starts and maybe that's how it ends.

It flows through us like strange wine, like poetry, like death and maybe one day we'll emerge on the other side, and it'll make a sort of sense or maybe we'll scratch our heads and wonder what the hell we were doing. Then perhaps the sun will shine, and we'll become something that's bigger than ourselves. Something with vibrancy, colour, poetry, and the wonders of the universe.

I hope your life is full of madness and daftness and beauty and poetry. I hope you get to see things that aren't there and that everything you once believed has become something else. Only then will you understand the ways of God and the universe.

All I've ever asked is for you to believe in my madness. All I've ever asked is for you to ascend into my chaos. All I've ever asked is for you to be baptised in my golden syrup. Yes, you'll emerge a bit sticky but think of all the wonders you'll see submerged beneath the gloop. It will turn you into a poetic lunatic who only lives for art. They'll either embrace you or send you off to a madhouse. It depends on which way the wind is blowing and the general attitude of society at the time.

Who is the Man Behind this Mystery?

This seems like a fairly interesting question. So one day a private detective, who had nothing better to do with his existence, decided to find out. Three days after that fateful one day, the detective was found trembling in a corner, crying piteously, his head clutched desperately in his hands, as if the very Devil had been implanted. A brief report on his desk read as follows:

"The man lurking behind the curtain of this bewitching phantasmagoria goes by the name of Joel Dean. He would dearly like to know what the hell is going on in the world but is finding it increasingly difficult to comprehend. One day he would like to become something he isn't. Only then will he fully grasp the mysteries of the universe. His hobbies include escaping, vanishing into thin air and making private detectives go mad."

Oh dear me, poor private detective! The warning signs were all there but in your foolish pride you ignored them. Sad to tell, the detective has never recovered, which is a shame really, when you think about it.

Printed in Poland
by Amazon Fulfillment
Poland Sp. z o.o., Wrocław

22253349R00049